LET'S BE FIREFIGHTERS!

Based on the teleplay "Fired Up!" by Gabe Pulliam

Adapted by Frank Berrios

Illustrated by Niki Foley

A GOLDEN BOOK • NEW YORK

© 2016 Viacom International Inc. All rights reserved. Published in the United States by Golden Books, an imprint of Random House Children's Books, a division of Penguin Random House LLC, 1745 Broadway, New York, NY 10019, and in Canada by Penguin Random House Canada Limited, Toronto. Golden Books, A Golden Book, A Little Golden Book, the G colophon, and the distinctive gold spine are registered trademarks of Penguin Random House LLC. Nickelodeon, Blaze and the Monster Machines, and all related titles, logos, and characters are trademarks of Viacom International Inc.
ISBN 978-0-399-55351-6
randomhousekids.com
T#: 469158
Printed in the United States of America
10 9 8 7 6 5 4 3 2

One morning, Blaze and his friends were doing awesome stunts at the Axle City Garage.

"Check this out!" Blaze shouted as he zoomed down a spiral slide.

Stripes went next, clinging to the edges of the slide with his clawed tires. He leapt off with a growl and landed beside his friends.

Pickle took a turn, giggling all the way down.

"Crusher, you have to try this," he said. "It's so much fun!"

"Be there in a second," replied Crusher. "I'm making a pizza!" He slipped the pie into the oven, then joined his friends.

A little while later, Stripes smelled something—
it was smoke! Suddenly, an alarm began to ring.
"That's the smoke alarm!" said Gabby. "It lets us
know there could be a fire!"

Blaze told his friends to stay calm. Then he formed a plan.

"Everybody line up and follow me," he said. He led everyone outside and counted to make sure they'd all gotten out safely.

"Hooray!" cheered Pickle. "Blaze got everyone outside, safe and sound!"

With sirens wailing, firefighters raced to the scene.
"This looks like an emergency!" the fire chief said
to the other fire engines. "Get your hoses ready and
follow me!"
The firefighters rolled into the smoky garage.

"Wow, those firefighters are so brave!" said Pickle.

"I wish I could be a firefighter someday," remarked Blaze.

"You'd make an awesome firefighter, Blaze," said AJ. "You're the bravest Monster Machine I know."

"Well, folks, we found what was making all that smoke," the chief said. "Looks like someone left their pizza in the oven too long."

"Hey, Crusher! Isn't that the pizza you were cooking?" asked Pickle.

"My pizza!" Crusher whined. "I can't eat it now!"

"Y'know, Blaze, I think you've got what it takes to be a firefighter yourself. First you'll need a firefighting badge," said the chief, and he gave Blaze a badge with four stars on it. "See these stars?" One of them began to shine. "Whenever you help out in an emergency, a star lights up. To become a firefighter, you'll need to earn all four stars."

Blaze smiled. After earning his first star at the garage, he was eager to do more!

Later that day, Blaze and AJ heard shouts coming from a yogurt factory. Inside, a pipe had burst, and a worker was trapped on top of a blasting stream of yogurt!

"We have to find some way to stop the yogurt from coming out of that broken pipe!" said AJ.

"We can use a valve to stop it!" said Blaze.

"A valve is like a door," Blaze explained. "When it's open, the yogurt can flow through the pipe. But when I close it, the yogurt stops flowing!"

AJ closed the valve, the yogurt stopped, and the worker was safe.

Another star lit up on Blaze's firefighter badge.

"I got another star for helping in an emergency!" he said. "Just two more and I'll be a firefighter!"

That afternoon, Blaze and AJ drove to the outskirts of Axle City, where they saw a flock of sheep that needed their help.

"A baby sheep is stuck in the quarry, and he doesn't know how to get out," said Blaze. "We have to rescue him! This is an emergency!"

Blaze hitched himself to an old mine cart, and the sheep hopped aboard. They set off down the rickety tracks.

"We're here, baby sheep!" said Blaze. All the sheep were reunited, and the baby sheep was happy.

As he pulled the sheep out of the quarry, a third star lit up on Blaze's firefighter badge.

"That's my third star!" exclaimed Blaze. "Just one more to go!"

As Blaze and AJ made their way back home, they heard sirens—and saw smoke!

"Lug nuts! It's a forest fire!" said Blaze. He also noticed that there were five fires, but only four firefighters!

"For an emergency this big, we need five fire engines working together!" said the fire chief. "Let's turn me into a fire engine!" Blaze told AJ.

"I'm a fire engine Monster Machine!" cried Blaze after his transformation.

"Awesome! Now let's go help those firefighters!" replied AJ.

"Fire engine Blaze reporting for duty! I'm ready to put out that fire!" said Blaze.

"Well, all right! Let's see what you've got!" said the chief.

Blaze and AJ raced to the fire. AJ opened the valve on the fire hose, and water blasted out. AJ aimed the water at the flames, and soon the fire was out!

Then one of the firefighters spotted more smoke.
"There's more fire down there!" he yelled.
"And it's heading for those trees!" called
another firefighter.

"Don't worry, Chief!" said Blaze. "I can stop the fire before it gets to the trees! I'll use Blazing Speed to get there super fast!"

Zoom! Blaze and AJ raced through the forest, putting out one fire after another until they were all gone!

Just as the other fire trucks caught up to Blaze and AJ, the fourth star lit up on Blaze's badge.

"Congratulations, Blaze!" the chief said proudly. "You've proven that you can handle any emergency." And with that, the chief handed Blaze his very own fire helmet.

"Let's hear it for Blaze, Axle City's newest firefighter!" exclaimed the chief, and all the engines cheered.